Stinky Spike
and the Royal Rescue

 **READ & BLOOM BOOKS**

Stinky Spike
and the Royal Rescue

Peter Meisel

illustrated by
Paul Meisel

BLOOMSBURY

NEW YORK   LONDON   OXFORD   NEW DELHI   SYDNEY

For Grand Marie and Papa Bob —Peter M.

For Cheryl —Paul M.

First published in the United States of America in March 2017
by Bloomsbury Children's Books
www.bloomsbury.com

Bloomsbury is a registered trademark of Bloomsbury Publishing Plc

For information about permission to reproduce selections from this book, write to
Permissions, Bloomsbury Children's Books, 1385 Broadway, New York, New York 10018
Bloomsbury books may be purchased for business or promotional use. For information on bulk
purchases please contact Macmillan Corporate and Premium Sales Department at
specialmarkets@macmillan.com

Library of Congress Cataloging-in-Publication Data
Names: Meisel, Peter, author. | Meisel, Paul, illustrator.
Title: Stinky Spike and the royal rescue / by Peter Meisel ; illustrated by Paul Meisel.
Description: New York : Bloomsbury, 2017. | Series: Read & bloom
Summary: Stinky Spike the dog and Captain Fishbeard the pirate are thick as thieves now that
Spike has proved his treasure-sniffing ability. When Spike and his crew come across a sign offering a
reward for finding the Princess's lost poodle, they can hardly resist. Surely finding a fluffy royal pooch
can't be very difficult? When blundering pirates are involved, things never go according to plan.
Identifiers: LCCN 2016024740 (print) | LCCN 2016036828 (e-book)
ISBN 978-1-61963-883-9 (hardcover) • ISBN 978-1-61963-884-6 (e-book) • ISBN 978-1-61963-885-3 (e-PDF)
Subjects: | CYAC: Dogs—Fiction. | Smell—Fiction. | Pirates—Fiction. | Humorous stories. | BISAC:
JUVENILE FICTION / Readers / Chapter Books. | JUVENILE FICTION / Animals / Dogs. | JUVENILE
FICTION / Action & Adventure / Pirates. | JUVENILE FICTION / Humorous Stories.
Classification: LCC PZ7.1.M469 Sq 2017 (print) | LCC PZ7.1.M469 (e-book) | DDC [Fic]—dc23
LC record available at https://lccn.loc.gov/2016024740

Art created using pencil on Strathmore Bristol and colored digitally
Typeset in Century Schoolbook
Book design by Yelena Safronova
Printed in China by C&C Offset Printing Co., Ltd., Shenzhen, Guangdong
1 3 5 7 9 10 8 6 4 2

All papers used by Bloomsbury Publishing, Inc., are natural, recyclable products
made from wood grown in well-managed forests. The manufacturing processes
conform to the environmental regulations of the country of origin.

Table of Contents

CHAPTER 1
CRASH LANDING

It was nap time on the pirate ship
Driftwood. Captain Fishbeard
and his crew had just feasted on
lumpfish stew and octopus pudding.
Now they were snoring and snorting
like thunder.

Stinky Spike slept on top of a steaming heap of moldy green cheese. He woofed in his sleep, chasing after skunks and stink-bats in his dreams.

Zip, the monkey pirate, was supposed to be looking out for enemy ships, strange creatures, and other dangers of the sea. But he was fast asleep too.

So nobody felt the mighty gust of wind catch the sails and send the *Driftwood* speeding toward shore!

CRAAAAACK! The sound of the crashing ship jolted the pirates wide awake.

"Shiver me timbers, we're under attack!" bellowed Captain Fishbeard.

"Yikes! Is it a sea monster?" cried Zelda, the first mate.

Spike scampered to the bow. *"Ah-roo!*

Ah-roo! It's no monster. We've crashed into a ship!"

Captain Fishbeard surveyed the damage. "*Arrrgh!* Zip, you lazy rascal. You fell asleep on the job and nearly sank our ship!"

From below roared a mighty voice, "My ship! My beautiful ship . . . she's ruined!"

The pirates scurried to the railing and looked down. Standing on a floating pile of timber was a small man wearing a crown. "You wretched pirates, look at what you've done!" he cried.

"*Arrrgh*, that's King Seabreeze, the ruler of Beeswax Island," whispered Captain Fishbeard.

"You bumbling buccaneers! You've shattered my favorite ship! I don't know if we'll ever be able to repair her," whimpered King Seabreeze.

He began to sniffle, then sob. Great tears ran down the king's cheek.

"Is the king *crying*?" whispered Zelda.

King Seabreeze wiped his nose on his royal sleeve. "NO! I am not crying. A king never cries!"

"*Arrrgh*, we can help you fix your ship," said Captain Fishbeard.

"Your Majesty, would you like some moldy green cheese? Rotten smells always cheer me up when I'm feeling sad," said Spike.

Before the king could answer, one of the guards called out, "Your Majesty, the Royal Pup is missing!"

"Princess Petunia will never forgive me if we've lost her beloved dog, Honey!" gasped the king.

"*Arrrgh*, we can help you find the pup," said Captain Fishbeard.

The king stamped his foot. "You fools have done enough. You've destroyed my ship and scared off

the princess's Royal Pup. Guards, seize them! Throw these stinking pirates into the dungeon!"

The king's guards rounded up the pirates and marched them through King Seabreeze's palace to the cold, dark dungeon. The pirates shivered as the guard locked the door to their cell.

"*Arrrgh*, we need to find a way out of this jail," said Captain Fishbeard.

Zip tried to squeeze through the bars. Spike tried to dig through the floor. Zelda even tried to pick the lock. It was no use. The pirates were trapped.

Days passed and still the pirates could not escape the king's dungeon. And a dungeon was no place to be stuck with Stinky Spike.

The globs of cheese, scraps of seaweed, and crab claws that were trapped in his fur had a mighty odor.

"Spike stinks worse than a buzzard's belch," exclaimed Zip.

The pirates tried to clean Spike.
They scrubbed him with wooden
spoons and tin cups. They
brushed his teeth with fish tails.
They bathed him in a bucket of
rain water.

"*Ah-roo, ah-roo*, that's enough," howled Spike. With a mighty shake, he sent gobs of moldy green cheese, crusty crab claws, and flaky fish scales flying in all directions. It was no use. The pirate crew could do nothing but pinch their noses to escape Spike's mighty stink.

That night, as the pirates tossed and turned, there was a noise outside the dungeon. Slowly, the door creaked open. A young girl stepped into the dark room.

"*Pssst. Pssst.* Wake up, you stinky pirates," whispered the girl.

"*Arrrgh*, who are you?" grumbled Captain Fishbeard.

"*Shhhhh* . . . I'm Princess Petunia. Is it true one of you has a super sniffer?" asked the princess.

"*Arrrgh*, it's true. Spike's the pup

you're after," whispered Captain
Fishbeard.

"*Yarf!* That's me," said Spike.

"Is your sniffer as powerful as
they say? Can you use it to find
anything?" asked Petunia.

"Yes, Your Highness. What's missing?" yipped Spike.

"Haven't you heard?" asked Petunia. "Ever since you pirates crashed into Daddy's ship, my pup has been missing. Her name is Honey, and she's my best friend. Can you help me find her?"

"Finding a missing dog will be easy for a sniffer like mine. I've got the most powerful nose on the seven seas," boasted Spike.

"I'll free you from this dungeon

so you can lead me to Honey. But we must be quick. If the king finds out my plan, he'll be very unhappy," said Petunia, holding her nose.

"*Arrrgh!* What about us? We can't rot in this dungeon forever," said Captain Fishbeard.

"If Spike finds Honey, the king will set you all free. I promise," said Petunia.

"*Arrrgh*, good luck, Spike. You're our only hope out of this mess," said Captain Fishbeard.

CHAPTER 2
THE SEARCH FOR HONEY

Princess Petunia and Stinky Spike tiptoed past the sleeping guards.

"We should start by searching the island," whispered Petunia.

"I'm one sniff ahead of you, Princess," said Spike. He pointed his nose into the air and took a deep breath.

Petunia pulled something out of her pocket and held it up to Spike's nose. "This is Honey's royal cloak. Use it to get her scent."

Spike took a deep sniff. "Aha! It smells like Honey is in the jungle. Follow me!" said Spike.

Spike stopped beneath a large tree. He put his nose to the ground and sniffed around the trunk.

"I think Honey is up in this tree," Spike whispered.

Spike barked, and clawed at the tree, "*Arf, Arf!* Honey, we're here to rescue you!"

"*Grrrrr*... Go away! And get your own honey," growled a voice from above.

A sticky drop fell out of the tree and onto Spike's nose. "*Ah-roo,* what is this strange-smelling stuff? It's stuck to my sniffer!" he howled. He could hear an unusual buzzing sound coming from above.

"Honey, come down from the tree right now. It's time to go home," commanded Petunia. She shook the tree.

The voice growled again from above, "Stop shaking the tree,

you'll wake the . . . BEES! Oh,
no . . . OUCH! They're stinging
me!" roared the voice from above.

THUD! A great big bear dropped
out of the tree and landed next to
Petunia.

"*Grrrrr*, I told you, that was my
honey. I was just about to get a
paw-full before you woke the hive.
Now buzz off, you troublemakers,"
said the bear.

"Sorry, Bear. We thought you

were my missing dog, Honey. Have you seen her?" asked Petunia.

"*Hmmm.* I know all about honey. But I don't know anything about a missing *dog* named Honey," said the bear, scratching his head. "I did see a scruffy mutt on the beach. Maybe it's the one you're looking for."

"Oh, thank you, Bear! Come on, Spike. I know the way to the beach," said Petunia.

"And sorry about your bee stings," said Spike, still trying to lick the sticky honey off his nose.

When they got to the beach,
Stinky Spike and Princess Petunia
looked up and down the shoreline.

"There's nothing here but sandy
seashells. Spike, do you smell
anything?" asked Petunia.

Spike took a deep sniff. "*Ah-roo!*

Wet dog! I'd know that scent anywhere. Honey must be nearby," howled Spike, dashing toward the dunes.

"*Arf, arf,*" barked Spike, pointing to a curled-up mutt sleeping behind a sand dune.

"*Ah-roo! Ah-roo!*" howled Spike. "Honey! We've found you."

Princess Petunia ran up beside Spike.

"That's not Honey," she said, stamping her royal foot.

"No. I'm Patches," said the shaggy dog, shaking sand from his coat. "Who's Honey?"

"Honey is Princess Petunia's pup," explained Spike.

"*Hmmm . . .* that name sounds

familiar," said Patches. The scrappy

pup thought for a second, then

began digging in the sand.

Suddenly he hit something.

CLINK!

Patches pulled a bottle from the hole. Then another. Then another.

"Maybe your friend Honey has been writing these notes," said Patches. Inside each bottle was a slip of paper. The princess pulled them out and read them one by one.

"I'd know Honey's paw print anywhere. These notes are from her! But who is Captain Bart?" asked Petunia.

"Captain Bart is a mean old

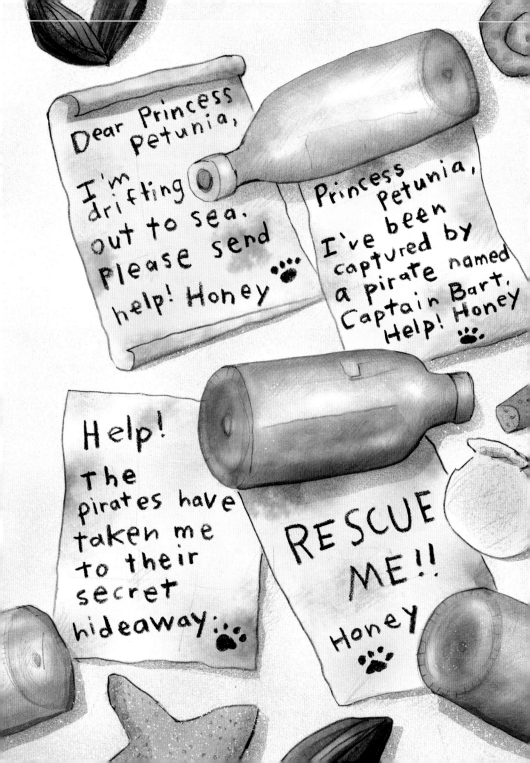

pirate. And his crew is even worse. But don't worry, Princess. My super sniffer will lead us right to Honey, and we will rescue her! All we need is a ship," said Spike.

"We can use my boat. She's rickety, but quick enough to chase after bonefish," offered Patches.

"*Yippee!* Off to find Honey we go," barked Spike.

Stinky Spike and Princess Petunia climbed aboard the

little boat. Patches raised the
sail and steered out to sea. Spike
stuck his mighty snout into the
breeze and took a deep *SNIFF* . . .
SNIFFFFFF . . .

"Aha! I smell pirates in that
direction," said Spike, pointing to
the horizon.

With his nose in the air and his tail wagging behind him, Spike shouted out directions to Patches, who steered the boat toward the pirates.

At last, Spike spotted a tiny island in the distance.

"*Ah-roo!* Land ho!" cheered Spike.

CHAPTER 3

RESCUE FROM THE PIRATES' HIDEOUT

As the boat sailed closer to shore, Spike saw that the beach was littered with pirate gear. Pirate pants and shirts flapped in the wind. Hats, flags, and sails were draped on the tree branches.

"This island is covered in pirate gear, but I don't see or smell any pirates. They must be hiding," said Spike.

Suddenly, a brightly colored parrot swooped at Spike. It was wearing a pirate hat!

"Hey! Watch where you're flying, feather-neck," barked Spike.

The parrot perched on the side of the boat and stared at Princess Petunia's necklace.

"*Caw!* That's a nice shiny necklace. Give it to me!" he squawked.

"First, tell me where all of this pirate gear came from. Is it from Captain Bart's crew?" asked Petunia.

"*Baccaw!* Hand over that shiny necklace," squawked the parrot, ignoring the princess's question.

"These must be the Pirate Parrots of Copycat Cove. They are a menace to sailors everywhere," said Patches.

"Shiny necklace! Shiny necklace!" squawked the parrot. Soon the masts were full of birds.

"Shiny necklace! Shiny necklace!" squawked the other parrots.

Princess Petunia had an idea. "Let's make a deal. You want shiny things, and I want my dog, Honey. But she was captured by

Captain Bart. I'll trade you my gold necklace if you take us to the pirates' hideout."

"*Buh-squawk!* Deal! Follow me,"
said the parrot.

Patches steered his boat after
the parrot. They sailed around the
island and into a hidden cove.
There, a pirate ship sat bobbing
in the waves.

"I see Honey! But

she's surrounded by Captain Bart and his crew. We need a plan to save her!" said Petunia.

Spike took a deep sniff. "If only I could smell us a plan that would save Honey. But it's hard to smell anything over all of these parrots."

"Aha, Spike, that's it! These birds

can help us distract the pirates," said Petunia.

"*Ah-roo*, great idea, Princess," howled Spike.

Patches anchored the ship, and Spike said, "Listen up, parrots. The necklace is yours! Now, how would you like to earn some more pirate gear?"

"*Buh-squawk!*" The parrots screeched with excitement.

The princess tossed her

necklace to the parrots. "We need you to swarm, buzz, swoop, peck, and swipe everything you can from the pirate crew."

"*Cuh-caw!* Sure thing, Princess," squawked the parrot.

"*Ah-roo*, then follow us, flappers,"

howled Spike, as he and Petunia

charged toward the pirate camp.

When they were close, Spike

barked, "Swarm!"

The great flock of seabirds flew

at the pirates. They dove after their

pirate hats. They pecked at their

pirate beards. They clawed at

their shiny silver buckles.

"*Arrrgh*, run for your lives,

pirates!" yelled Captain Bart as

he ran into the jungle.

Petunia and Spike snuck into the
pirate camp. Honey was nowhere
to be found.

"Honey, Honey, where are you?"
called the princess.

"Leave it to me! My super sniffer
will find her now," said Spike.

Spike put his nose to the sky.
Sniff . . . sniff . . . sniff . . . "Well,

this is strange. I don't smell any dogs. But we know that Honey was just here," whimpered Spike.

"She must be here somewhere! I saw her," said Petunia.

"*Ah-roo!* I still can't smell her over all of these parrots," said Spike.

"We are running out of time. Captain Bart and his crew of awful pirates will come back to their camp and find us!" cried Petunia.

"Sorry, Princess, I don't smell Honey. But, I do smell cheese. *Cheese-ah-roo!* I'm hungry enough to eat Captain Bart's entire cheese supply," said Spike.

"Oh, no you're not. I command you to forget about cheese and to find Honey!" said Petunia.

But the rumbling of his stomach was too much for Spike. He trotted over to the pirates' campfire and inspected their abandoned feast.

"*Mmmm*, crab claws! *Yum!* Dried

mackerel," said Spike. "*Ahhh!*
Moldy cheese," he drooled, moving
the lid off a large barrel.

"*Ruff!*" A very stinky dog jumped
out of the barrel.

"Honey?" asked Spike. "*Ah-roo,
ah-roo*, Princess, we've found her!"

"Honey, it's you, at long last,"
said Petunia, wrapping her arms
around her pup in a great big hug.
Honey wagged her tail and licked
Princess Petunia's cheek.

The princess held her nose. "I'm

so glad you're safe, but what was in that barrel? You stink like a . . ."

"Not now, Princess Petunia. We have to go before the pirates get a whiff of us. Let's scram and take this barrel of rotten cheese for later," barked Spike.

Rolling the barrel between them, the princess, Spike, and Honey ran down the beach.

"This is one heavy barrel of cheese," Spike panted.

They rounded the beach to where
Patches was waiting in his boat.

"Patches, quickly set the sails.
We've got to make a fast escape,"
yelled Petunia.

Quickly they loaded the barrel into the little boat, jumped in, and set sail.

Spike nibbled on stinky cheese. Suddenly his tooth struck something hard.

"What do we have here?" wondered Spike, pulling a gold coin into view.

Honey grinned. "It's Captain Bart's treasure! He keeps it hidden under this moldy cheese so the Pirate Parrots don't steal it. When the birds caused all the madness, I realized that this barrel would make a very good hiding spot. To thank you for saving me, the treasure is yours, Patches and Spike," said Honey.

"Hurray for treasure!" cried Patches.

"And hurray for CHEESE!" howled Spike with glee.

When the little crew landed back on Beeswax Island, King Seabreeze ran to meet them.

"Petunia! You're safe," cried the happy king. "And, Honey! You're found! But wow, you STINK!" he yelled, scratching the pup's ears.

"Daddy, I promised Spike that if

64

he helped me find Honey, we would release the pirate crew of the *Driftwood*," said Princess Petunia.

"Well, a promise is a promise," said the happy king.

He sent the guards to release the crew.

To celebrate Honey's safe return, King Seabreeze hosted a giant party!

"Princess Petunia, Patches, and Stinky Spike, you are heroes. You brought Honey home safe and sound. Spike, in your honor we have a feast of delicious—and stinky—treats!" announced the king.

"*Arrrgh*, Spike, you've saved us too. Thank you from the bottom of my pirate heart," said Captain Fishbeard.

"*Arf!* I have a present for you, Captain Fishbeard," said Spike, nudging the barrel toward Captain Fishbeard.

Zelda held her nose, "Ugh, this is no treasure. It's just moldy cheese."

Spike howled with laughter. "Look in the cheese. It's Captain Bart's treasure!"

"Aha, Captain Bart's treasure! More than enough to fix up the *Driftwood*!" shouted Captain Fishbeard, dancing a jig.

"Yo-ho-ho!" shouted the *Driftwood*'s crew.

Petunia giggled. "What an adventure this has been! Honey, we should form a pirate crew of our own. We can be the Princess Pirates!"

READ & BLOOM

PLANT THE LOVE OF READING!

Agnes and Clarabelle are the best of friends!

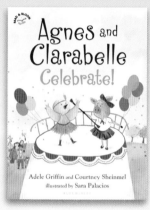

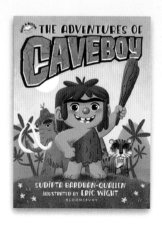

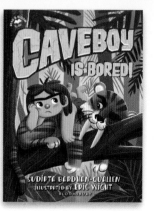

Caveboy is always ready for an adventure!

You don't want to miss these great characters! The Read & Bloom line is perfect for newly independent readers. These stories are fully illustrated and bursting with fun!

Stinky Spike can sniff his way out of any trouble!

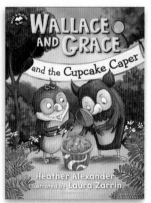

Wallace and Grace are owl detectives who solve mysteries!

Peter Meisel has been writing and illustrating since he was old enough to hold a crayon. He lives in Brooklyn, New York. *Stinky Spike the Pirate Dog* and *Stinky Spike and the Royal Rescue* are his first two children's books.

Paul Meisel lives in Newtown, Connecticut, with his wife and labradoodle, Coco, who was the inspiration for his two early readers, *See Me Dig* and the Geisel Honor–winning *See Me Run*. Paul is also the author/illustrator of *Good Night, Bat! Good Morning, Squirrel!* and has illustrated more than 70 books, including the bestselling I Can Read *Go Away, Dog*; *Run for Your Life!: Predators and Prey on the African Savanna*; and several Let's-Read-and-Find-Out Science books.

www.paulmeisel.com